How I Did It!

Written by Linda Ragsdale

Illustrated by Anoosha Syed

Silver Dolphin

In a classroom, surrounded by characters,
I stood straight and tall. I was proud.

I glanced to the right and thought,
If I tipped myself down, I could easily be H.

I was full of ideas.

Then I looked left and saw the most amazing thing!
Oh, I thought, *J is so well-rounded. I could do that.*

So I tried.

"Hey," harrumphed H. "What's happening here?"
"I just want to try to curve like J," I said.
"Hah," harped H.

J jibed,

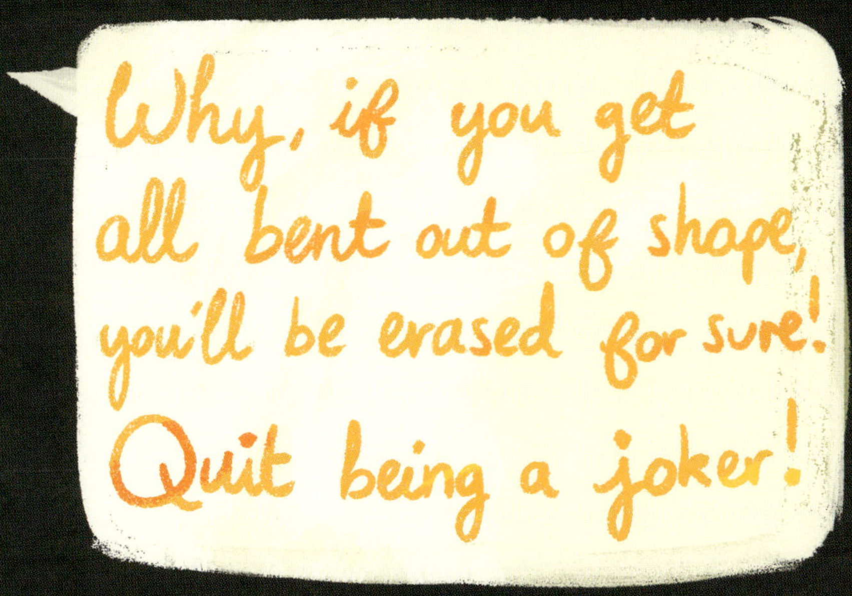

Why, if you get all bent out of shape, you'll be erased for sure! Quit being a joker!

Joker?!

"I can change if I choose. I'm not written in ink!"

I could not stand still for a moment longer.

I wrangled.

I tangled.

I yanked on the lines and... POP!

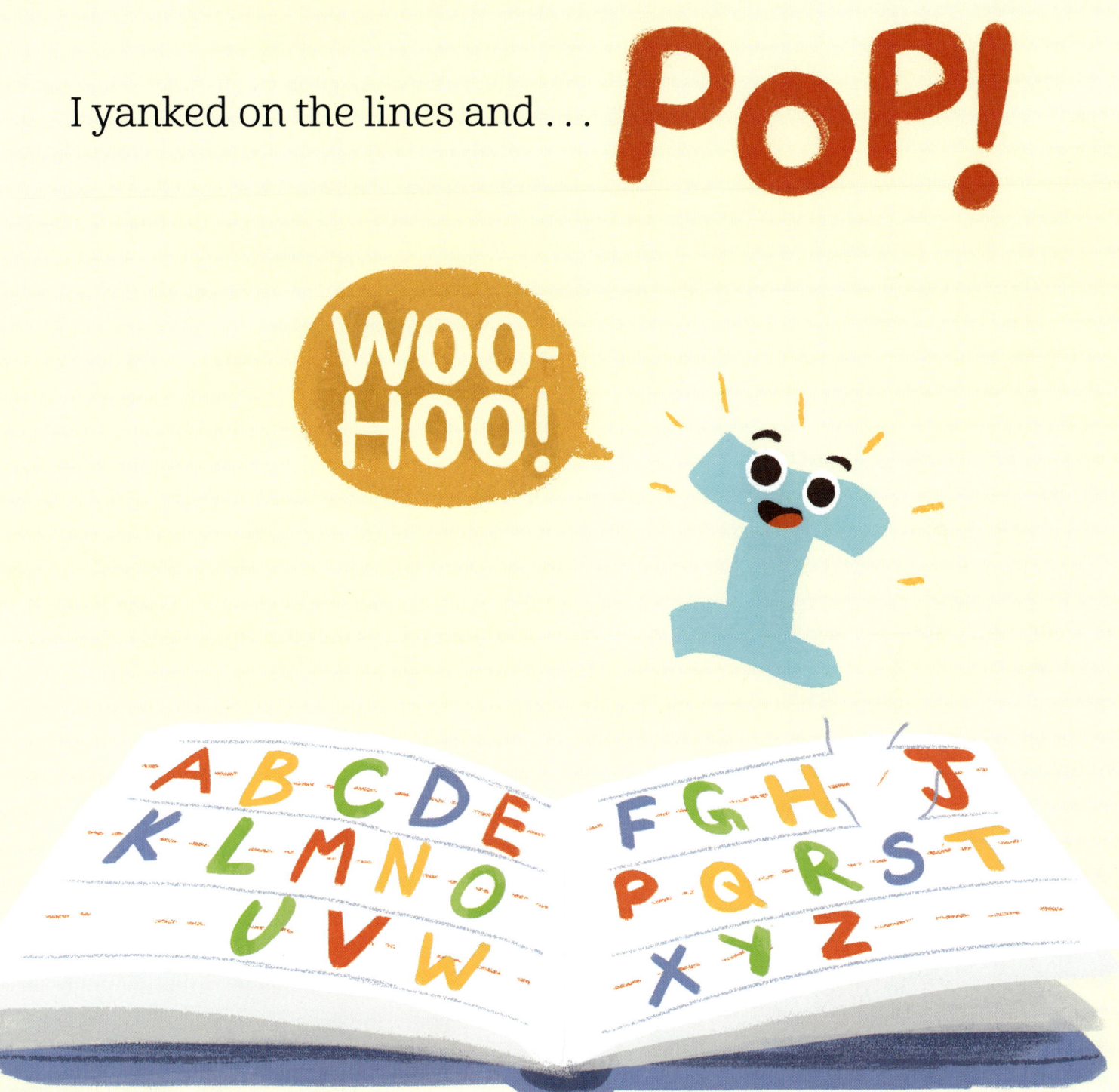

I broke free with a loud exclamation!

Wriggling like an inchworm,
I squirmed and scrunched between the lines.

I had a whole new point of view.

E yelled, "TAKE it EASY!"

F frowned over the fuss.

"Good Grief!" gasped G.

"Ooooh," said O. "Outstanding!"

T was tickled.

"What's wrong with wandering?"

wondered W.

"THAT IS REALLY CROSSING THE LINES!"

exclaimed X.

As I reached for new heights,
A saw what C saw,
and they could not believe what I was doing!

B just let it be.

I ignored them all. I kept going.

In the middle of a scrunch, I stood up.
I began to walk, then run.
I leapt, skipped, and danced along the dashed lines.

I was really on the move!
But I was too excited to notice . . .

I didn't see it coming.
The trouble ahead.
The end of the line.

That's when I fell.

I was a mess. Crumpled and twisted.
I felt like nothing more than a scribble.
I didn't move. I couldn't move.
I didn't know where I started or ended.

"You should have minded your p's and q's and stayed in the lines," pompously quipped P and Q.

"So sad . . ." sighed S.

S was right. I *was* so sad.

I curled up into a ball. I wasn't going to take any more chances. I was done. This was it. Period.

Or was I? I took a good look.
I realized... I *was* well-rounded!

I was not done.
I had so much more to do.
I had so many more things to try.
If I focused on flipping, I flipped.
If I wanted, I could curl, swirl, twist, and turn.

I could do anything. I could be anything.
Anything I wanted to be.
Anything all the way from A to Z.
I was full of possibilities!

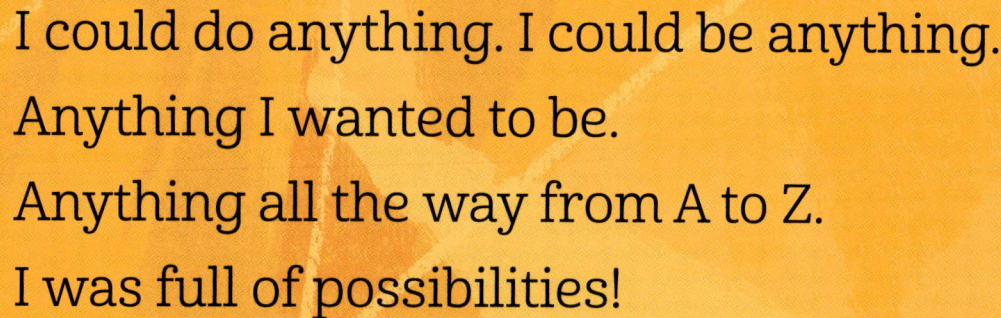

I was ready to explore them all.
I knew I could do it!

Just as I was about to head off on a new adventure, I looked up and I saw U.
And I knew . . .

U could do it too.